GIRLZROCK!

School Play Stars

Julie Mullins

illustrated by
Monika Maddock

MONDO

InclusionSE

First published in 2005 by
MACMILLAN EDUCATION AUSTRALIA PTY LTD
627 Chapel Street, South Yarra, Australia 3141

This edition first published in the United States of America
in 2005 by MONDO Publishing.

For information contact:
MONDO Publishing
980 Avenue of the Americas
New York, NY 10018

Visit our web site at http://www.mondopub.com

05 06 07 08 09   9 8 7 6 5 4 3 2 1

ISBN 1-59336-706-6 (PB)

Library of Congress Cataloging-in-Publication Data

Mullins, Julie.
   School play stars / Julie Mullins ; illustrated by Monika Maddock.
      p. cm. – (Girlz rock!)
   Summary: Best friends Jules and Rosa try out for the school play and are
   surprised when the reluctant Jules gets the lead. Includes extra sections with
   facts, vocabulary, questions, jokes, and more.
   ISBN 1-59336-706-6 (pbk.)
    [1. Theater—Fiction. 2. Schools—Fiction. 3. Best friends—Fiction. 4.
   Friendship—Fiction.] I. Maddock, Monika, ill. II. Title. III. Series.

   PZ7.M9212Sch 2005
   [Fic]—dc22

                                                            2005043880

Series created by Felice Arena and Phil Kettle
Project Management by Limelight Press Pty Ltd
Cover and text design by Lore Foye
Illustrations by Monika Maddock

Printed in Hong Kong

Contents

Rosa   *Jules*

CHAPTER 1

It's On!

Rosa runs across the school playground toward her best friend, Jules, who is sitting under a tree eating her lunch.

Rosa "Jules! Hey, look over there! It's finally up!"

Jules "What's up?"

Rosa "The notice about the school play. Come on!"

Rosa rushes back to the main school building with Jules only a few steps behind. The girls run over to a noticeboard that's outside the teachers' staff room. The notice reads:

This year's school play auditions will be held at lunchtime tomorrow in Mr. Tuttle's classroom.

Rosa "Great, the auditions are with Mr. Tuttle. He's pretty cool so this year's play will be something funky, I bet. What are you gonna do for your audition, Jules?"

Jules "Um, I dunno. I get really nervous about all that stuff."

Rosa "Yeah, me too, but it'll be really cool once we get into it!"

Jules "I guess so. I'd really like an acting part but I just can't sing that well. I sound more like a goose with a bad cold."

Rosa "No, you don't. And anyway, no one says you have to sing. We don't even know yet if there's music in it."

Jules "Oh, okay then. I can always be a tree and wave my lovely leaves around silently—boring!"

Rosa "It'll be fine—you'll see. This'll be the best school play ever!"

CHAPTER 2

The Audition

The next day, Rosa and Jules are
waiting with some other children
outside Mr. Tuttle's classroom.
After a few minutes Mr. Tuttle lets
everyone in. He asks them to sit
down and wait for him to call them.

Rosa "Gee, I feel really nervous
now. But I guess it's normal to feel
like that. Some actors say it even
helps them perform better."

Jules "I once heard that a guy from another school was so nervous when he walked out on stage that he wet himself. He was dressed as a pineapple and he had this huge stain down his front that everyone could see."

Rosa giggles.

Jules "Imagine if that happened to me—I'd just die!"

Rosa "Yeah, it'd be *so* embarrassing...but it won't happen. We'll be okay. This is our big chance to be school play stars. If we're really nervous, we can just think of the principal doing something really dumb. Then we'll forget all about being scared."

Jules "Yeah! Thanks, I'll keep that in mind. What do you think Mr. Tuttle will make us do?"

Rosa "Well, we might have to read something or else pretend to be something weird. Or maybe he'll ask us to do some dance moves or sing a little."

Jules "Sing? I don't think so!"

Rosa "Well, I don't know. I'm just saying we might have to try different things, that's all."

Jules "Maybe this isn't such a good idea—I don't feel so good."

Rosa "Don't be a wimp! You'll be all right. You never know what might happen. Look, it's our turn next. Mr. Tuttle is waving us in."

Jules "Oh, no! I'm busting. I need to go really bad."

Rosa "Too late for that. Just hold on. We're in this together, remember."

CHAPTER 3

Hip-hop Porridge

The next day, Mr. Tuttle tells Jules and Rosa that they have both been chosen to be in the play. He tells them that the performance will be *The Three Bears*, hip-hop style.

Jules "I just can't believe I got the lead role! My singing must've been okay after all. I hope I make a cool Goldilocks. I think I'll wear a wig so I'll look like Avril. What do you think? Rosa? What's wrong?"

Rosa "Nothing."

Jules "You sure?"

Rosa "This whole thing sucks! How come you get the main part and all I get to be is a dumb bowl of porridge? You didn't even want to try out in the first place."

Jules "Yeah, but you won't be just any bowl of porridge. You'll be the one that's 'not too hot, not too cold, but just right.' And from what Mr. Tuttle says, you'll be the best hip-hopping bowl of porridge ever!"

Rosa "Yeah, well it's still not as good as Goldilocks."

Jules "If you're that bummed out I can ask Mr. Tuttle to swap us. I'm still scared that I might lose it in front of the audience. How awful would that be? They'd call me Goldi*lost* instead of Goldil*ocks*!"

Rosa "Thanks for the offer, Jules, but I'll stick with being porridge. You'll be great as Goldilocks."

Jules suddenly has a thought.

Jules "Wait here, I've got an idea."

Before Rosa can say anything, Jules races across the playground toward the staff room.

CHAPTER 4

Dying to Get On

A few minutes later, Jules returns
to where Rosa is sitting in the
playground.

Jules "I asked Mr. Tuttle if you can learn everyone else's parts, just in case someone gets sick and can't go on the night of the show. He thinks it's a great idea and said you should come to practice. Please, please, please do it!"

Rosa "Yeah, okay."

Jules "Cool! Mr. Tuttle wants us to write our own hip-hop lyrics, so we can write the words for Goldilocks together—you'll be way better at it than me."

Rosa "And he said I can learn all the main parts, right? Mama, Papa, and Baby Bear, your part, and the chairs?"

Jules "Yup!"

Rosa "Cool! Imagine if someone really does get sick the night of the show and can't do it. But it probably won't happen. Everyone wants to be in the play too much. They'd be dying and still go on!"

Jules "Well, you never know. Billy Cooper is always getting sick. Remember when he came to school with huge red spots all over his face?"

Rosa "Oh, yeah, that was totally gross! And he had like a million lice jumping off his head."

Jules (her fingers creeping up Rosa's arm) "Ew! See, you never know what creepy-crawly might be hanging around, just waiting to pounce!"

Rosa (screaming) "Ahh, yuck! Get lost!"

CHAPTER 5

The Big Night

It's Friday night and the parents and
friends of all the kids in the play are
going to their seats in the school hall.

Backstage, teachers are calling out, "Next for makeup! Jamie to wardrobe!" Jules is dressed as a hip-hop Goldilocks and Rosa as a bowl of porridge. Suddenly Mr. Tuttle appears and whispers something in Rosa's ear. Jules rushes over.

Jules "What's going on, Rosa?"

Rosa "You're not gonna believe it! Rebecca Allan's mother just phoned to say Rebecca's got a tummy bug and can't get out of bed, and Mr. Tuttle wants me to play her part—Papa Bear!"

Jules "That's great! I mean, bad for Rebecca but really cool for you."

Rosa "Mr. Tuttle said when my bowl of porridge scene is over I have to change quickly into the Papa Bear costume."

Jules "Great! That's my favorite part, especially when you'll have to growl!"

Rosa "But what about all the people out there? What if I forget the words or the beat?"

Jules "If you get nervous just do what we said."

Rosa "What d'you mean?"

Jules "You know, just imagine the
   principal doing something dumb!"
Rosa "Oh, yeah, that's right."

Rosa takes a peek through the
curtains and looks out at the
audience, all waiting. She smiles
and begins to get excited.

Rosa (turning back to Jules) "Hey, Jules, it's time. Break a leg!"

Jules "You too. Good luck!"

As the lights dim, hip-hop music starts booming through the school hall. All the actors take their places with Jules center stage. Then it's on with the show! Before they know it, it's time to take a bow.

Jules (whispering to Rosa) "Y'know Rosa, I wouldn't have been Goldilocks if it wasn't for you. We're both school play stars now!"

Rosa "You bet!"

After three encores, the curtain falls as the audience claps loudly for the last time. Everyone comments to each other how great the kids were— definite stars in the making!

Jules

GiRLZROCK!
School Play
Lingo

Rosa

break a leg An expression said to actors before they go on stage that wishes them good luck with their performance. It doesn't mean that they should fall off the stage and break their leg!

curtain call At the end of a performance when the actors come out on stage through the closed curtains and take a bow.

encore A French word that means "again." People in the audience shout it out at the end of a live performance when they want the performance to continue.

stage manager The person who is in charge of everything that happens on stage, including the lighting and props.

School Play Musts

☆ Be sure you've memorized your lines—it's embarrassing to be on stage with nothing to say!

☆ Don't forget to put on your stage makeup—bright stage lights make everyone look pale and washed out, and makeup helps the actors look better.

☆ Be sure to put your costume on properly. How bad would it be if it fell off while you were on stage!

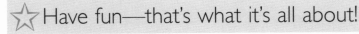
☆ Have fun—that's what it's all about!

☆ Invite your friends and family to the play you are in so there are people in the audience to cheer for you at the end.

☆ Learn how to sign your name in a really cool way—when you become a famous actress you'll have to sign lots of autographs!

☆ Practice making different faces and expressions in front of a mirror. This is sort of like having different roles in a play and it will help you become a better actress!

☆ Don't let a good performance go to your head—no one likes a conceited actress.

School Play Instant Info

The English writer William Shakespeare (1564–1616) is the most famous playwright in history. He wrote dozens of famous plays, like *Romeo and Juliet* and *Hamlet*, that are still being performed all over the world.

The stage manager sits backstage, usually on the left side of the stage (where the audience can't see him or her). This area is often called the "prompt corner," because in the olden days when an actor forgot what to say, the stage manager sitting there would whisper out the lines and prompt the actor.

The actress Katherine Hepburn (1907–2003) won more Best Actress Oscar Awards—four total—than any other actor. She was nominated 12 times!

The youngest girl ever to be nominated for a Best Actress Oscar was 13-year-old Keisha Castle-Hughes for her role in the 2003 movie *Whale Rider*.

The longest applause after a live performance took place in 1991 in Vienna, Austria. The audience clapped for one hour and 20 minutes—there were 101 curtain calls!

Think Tank

1 What parts do Jules and Rosa get in the school play?

2 Why does Rosa end up getting to play the part of Papa Bear?

3 What is an audition?

4 If you have butterflies in your stomach what does that mean?

5 "Rehearse" is another word for what?

6 How do you think Rosa feels when she finds out that Jules got the lead in the play? Why do you think she feels this way?

7 What do you think would have happened between Rosa and Jules if Rosa hadn't gotten to be Papa Bear?

8 Have you ever gotten nervous during a performance or audition? What did you do to calm yourself down?

Answers

1. Jules gets the part of Goldilocks and Rosa gets the part of a bowl of porridge.
2. Rosa ends up getting to be Papa Bear because the girl who is supposed to play this part gets sick and can't perform.
3. An audition is when you try out for a part in any performance—a play, film, TV show, or musical.
4. Having butterflies in your stomach means you're nervous. Professional actors say having a few butterflies helps you perform better.
5. "Rehearse" is another word for "practice."
6. Answers will vary.
7. Answers will vary.
8. Answers will vary.

How did you score?

- If you got most of the answers correct, then look out—a star is born! You love being in plays and dream of a career in show biz!

- If you got more than half of the answers correct, you like acting and with hard work might be able to star in a school play.

- If you got less than half of the answers correct, you probably prefer watching plays to acting in them.

Hey, Girls!

I have lots of fun reading books and plays. Sometimes I imagine I'm acting in a big theater—I close my eyes and picture what the setting and costumes look like.

I don't have a favorite play but I think it would be so much fun to get to sing and dance! My family and friends could be in the front row and they could all clap at the end of my performance!

You can make reading fun, too, by acting out the stories you read. Here are some ideas for making "School Play Stars" fun to read.

Find some costumes (or make some) for Goldilocks and the bowl of porridge. Use chairs as props and choose some good background music. So...have you decided who is going to be Rosa and who is going to be Jules? And what about the narrator?

Now act out the story in front of your friends—I'm sure you'll all have a great time! You also might like to take this story home and get someone in your family to read it with you. Maybe they can take on a part in the story.

So make sure you have fun reading. Books are like adventures—you just don't know where the next one will take you!

And remember, Girlz Rock!

When We Were Kids

Julie

Holly

Julie talked with Holly, another *Girlz Rock!* author

Julie "Were you ever in a school play, Holly? My favorite part was Maria in *The Sound of Music.*"

Holly "Yeah, I was Dorothy in *The Wizard of Oz.*

Julie "Imagine if we did a play together. I'd be Maria and you'd be Dorothy."

Holly "Yeah, and we could call it *The Wizard of Music.*"

Julie "Or *The Sound of Oz!*"

Holly "Or, I know…*The Girls from Oz* starring Julie and Holly."

Julie "Now you're talking. That's my kinda play!"

GIRLZROCK!
What a Laugh!

Q Why did the actress jump off the stage before the performance?

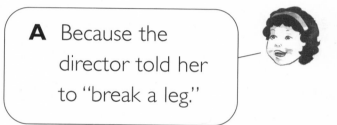

A Because the director told her to "break a leg."